Balboa Press books may be ordered through booksellers or by contacting:

Balboa Press
A Division of Hay House
1663 Liberty Drive
Bloomington, IN 47403
www.balboapress.com
844-682-1282

All images illustrated by: Elena Zabala

ISBN: 979-8-7652-5646-6 (sc)
ISBN: 979-8-7652-5645-9 (e)

Print information available on the last page.

Balboa Press rev. date: 11/27/2024

BALBOA.PRESS
A DIVISION OF HAY HOUSE

Book Intro

Welcome to *Jimmy and Max's Adventure: The Miracle*, a story full of surprises and the unexpected twists life brings when we least expect it. In our first book, *Jimmy and Max's Adventure: Escaping the City*, we joined these two friends on a journey that revealed the magic of true friendship. Along the way, they met new friends—some who became dear companions, and others who left behind treasured memories. Through their adventures, we learned the power of kindness, sharing joy, and the beauty of friendships that stand the test of time.

Now, get ready for another heartwarming chapter in Jimmy and Max's journey. This time, they're setting off on an adventure filled with fun, lessons, and love. In *The Miracle*, we discover the joy of welcoming new friends who truly care and the wisdom that comes from listening to those who've been through life's journeys before us. As you follow along, you'll see how opening your heart to the world brings new and wonderful experiences, and how those who walk beside you make every adventure even more special.

So, come join Jimmy and Max as they set off on this exciting new journey. We can't wait for you to discover *The Miracle* alongside them!

Dedication

To my husband and son, whose unwavering support through countless hours of stories and ideas has made this journey possible. Living with a children's storyteller isn't easy, but your patience and encouragement have been invaluable.

To my daughter Adriana, my rock, and to James and Zaine, who inspired Jimmy and Max.

To my dear friends, Rosemary and Christine, thank you for your help in editing and bringing these stories to life. Your love and friendship are truly priceless.

Contents

CHAPTER 1

The Story of Louie and Dora

They lived in a beautiful building on Main Street in a bustling city. Louie and Dora were neighbors and would often meet in the elevator on their way to the park across the street. They spent their days climbing branches and sitting in their favorite cherry blossom tree. They promised each other eternal love, but fate had its own plans.

Louie's parents decided to move to another city. He couldn't believe it. "How could they do this to us?" He looked around, noticing everything in his home was getting packed into boxes, including his bed and toys.

He had to do something. He needed to see Dora; he couldn't bear the thought of breaking their promise. He planned to escape, but just as he was ready to run, his father grabbed him and put him inside a traveling box, saying, "Oh no, you're not running away."

He cried and cried, but no one came to let him out. Before he knew it, he was on a plane traveling to a different city. He had no idea where he was being taken.

Meanwhile, back in the city, Dora was excited. She had been to the vet and learned she was going to be a mom. She eagerly went to the park every day, waiting for Louise, not knowing Louie was gone.

Nine weeks passed, and Dora gave birth to two beautiful kittens, that she named Jimmy and Max. They brought her joy, but tragedy struck when they fell from an open window. No one was there to save them, and Dora searched the city in vain.

During their many long conversations at the park, Dora and Louie often dreamed about the freedom of living in the forest. Little did they know that so many adventures would take place in the forest.

Louie wished with all of his heart that she would find happiness, even if it meant not finding him. His internal struggle continued, fueled by a deep longing. In the silent conversations with himself, he held onto the hope that one day their paths would cross again.

Louie thought about his future, and an idea echoed in his mind. "I do have nine lives, you know!" With a flicker of hope, he held onto the belief that maybe, in one of those lives, their story would take a different turn, and wishing once again to be a part of Dora's life and love.

A few years had gone by, Dora, Jimmy, and Max had traveled all over the country. They were free to explore the cat world where everything seemed so big for their small stature. One beautiful spring day, they came across a campsite with a blue camper displaying a delicious apple pie in the window. Enchanted by the aroma, Dora cautioned her boys about bears. Bears are notorious for wandering around campsites sniffing for food.

The beautiful lady called out, "Louie, go outside! Stop being so lazy, dear boy!"

Dora couldn't believe her ears! Was this a dream? Was the handsome black and white cat her Louie? Overwhelmed, she struggled to stand, confusing Jimmy and Max.

The boys were concerned and asked, " Mom what's the matter?"

Dora admitted, "My dears, I know that cat."

She revealed the painful past of Louie, their father, who had stopped coming to their meetings in the park before they were born. Despite the pain, she never stopped believing they would reunite. Jimmy and Max urged their mom to talk to Louie.

"Mama, please go and talk to him, he looks very sad", Said Jimmy.

Meanwhile, Louie was sitting on a tree branch, looking lost in thought and unhappy. Dora approached him slowly, while calling his name softly. "Louie! It's that You?"

Louie recognized the voice, turning to see Dora. The world stopped for a second, and no words were needed. They hugged, purred, and cried of happiness. True love has no ending and needs no explanations.

Dora said proudly, "Louie, these are your children, Jimmy and Max." Louie was so excited, happy and filled with joy. He couldn't wait to introduce them to his human parents Judy and Jose.

They all walked together back to the camper.

Judy said. "Louie, is this your family? Is this the beautiful cat, Dora from our old building? They look just like the two of you. This is a miracle!"

Louie was so happy to discover that he was a Papa that he pranced around the campsite with pride, excitement, and Love.

"Jose, I believe our family of three has now rapidly grown to 6," Judy said, smiling.

They were welcomed to their new home. From that moment, Dora, Louie, Jimmy, and Max began their happily-ever-after.

While they visited every corner of the campsite, Dora, Jimmy, and Max talked all about the time they traveled. They explained to Louie about their amazing adventures, and new friends they made along the way, and so much more.

They were once again ready to travel and this time Louie would be joining them. He didn't want to break Judy and Jose's heart by just leaving, so he decided to try to communicate his decision to them. Louie climbed onto Judy's lap and began to purr and sigh, and Judy understood what he was trying to tell her.

Judy said to Louie, "Louie, are you telling me that you'd like to go with your family? I'll tell you what, I think you really deserve to follow your dream. We will always be around here during springtime so you will know where to find us. Go with your family and have an amazing adventure."

Judy understood with compassion and love that she had to let him go. She took out her camera to capture a picture of Louie and his family finally reunited, she could not hold the happy tears in her eyes.

And that's how Jimmy and Max's adventure "The Miracle" began. Meow.

How might you feel finding out about a family member that you didn't know existed?

Cast of Characters:
Jimmy - Brave cat
Max - Cautious cat
Dora - Jimmy and Max's mom
Louie - Jimmy and Max's dad
Judy - Louie's caregiver mom
Jose - Louie's caregiver dad

CHAPTER 2

Happy Travels

The camp site was near a beautiful river, and Jimmy and Max were super excited to show their dad how they climb trees and feel the breeze hitting their fur. This was going to be an amazing adventure. Louie was used to being given food and a nice cozy place to sleep, so this was going to be a different kind of life, but sometimes change is great and can teach us so much.

Jimmy, Max, and Dora could not stop telling Louie about all of their friends and how they cared for each other. For Louie, this was all new because he had lived a very different life surrounded by his human parents and everything was given to him without even asking for it. The first night out in the woods, Louie was a bit scared and found himself shivering; he had never spent the night out of his lovely house. He had no idea of the noises that the night would bring, but he felt oddly safe with the enormous love and security that the boys were showing him.

"Dad, you will learn so much," said Jimmy.

Morning was arriving nice and slow, and since it was spring, the flowers were blooming everywhere.

"I have never seen anything so beautiful," said Louie. "Oh, Dad! You will love your new life," said Max.

Meanwhile they spotted a ship that was docked by the river and instantly desired to go for a trip.

"Wait, hold up! You're telling me we're going on that thing?" Louie exclaimed, his voice was full of uncertainty. "I mean, I've been in a cage on a plane, but never on a boat? That's a whole different story!"

The boat grew larger as it neared the shore. "Are you sure this is a good idea? What if I get seasick? What if I fall overboard? Or worse, what if it turns into a cat-napping cruise halfway through? " he continued, his tail flicking nervously.

Despite his fears, Louie couldn't deny the excitement radiating from Dora, Jimmy and Max. With a hesitant sigh, he squared his shoulders and prepared himself for this new adventure.

"Well, I guess there's a first time for everything," he muttered, trying to muster up some courage. "Just promise me one thing – no cages this time! I hope they have a litter box on board!"

As the boat came into view, Jimmy, Max, and Dora excitedly pointed it out to Louie.

"Look, Dad! That's our ticket to adventure!" exclaimed Jimmy, while Max added,

"Yeah, Dad, it's like a giant floating litter box... without the litter!" But his fears were quickly eased as the group explained the plan. "Don't worry, Louie," Dora reassured him, "we just have to be sneaky and blend in with the tourists. Besides, what could possibly go wrong on a colorful party boat like this?"

With a mixture of excitement and nervousness they found a safe spot to hop aboard, relieved to discover it was indeed a tour boat and not a cat-napping vessel in disguise. As they settled in, Louie couldn't help but marvel at the lively atmosphere.

"Well, I'll be whiskered! This is nothing like I expected," he remarked, watching people dancing and music filling the air.

With no idea where the ship was headed, they waved off the uncertainty, knowing that as long as they were together, they were ready for whatever adventure came their way. "Who cares where we're going when we're surrounded by good company and a boatload of fun?" Jimmy joked with a smile, and they all nodded in agreement, ready to set sail into the unknown.

They all jumped and hid in what looked like a laundry room at the bottom of the ship. Louie looked scared, but the confidence of Jimmy and Max gave him peace.

"Okay, I will follow you guys to the end of the world," said Louie.

"That's okay, Dad!" said Max. "We don't always know what to do. I was so scared of the forest and all of the decisions that Jimmy took while escaping the city. But now I have grown to be strong and adventurous…most of the time. It's ok to be scared"

Jimmy and Max knew that being sneaky and quiet was the most effective way to move around.

The abundance of food on the ship excited them, making their eyes wide with anticipation. They longed for city food and were confident they would have a feast.

Meow for now!

To where would you like to take a family trip?

Cast of Characters:
Jimmy - Brave Cat
Max - Cautious Cat
Dora - Jimmy and Max's Mom
Louie - Jimmy and Max's Dad

CHAPTER 3

Hiding in Plain Sight

They were aware that four cats on a ship would be challenging, but they believed that taking turns and only allowing one cat at a time would make it possible to fool the passengers. They were confident that the passengers would never realize there was more than one cat. It would be an incredibly sneaky and fun trick to pull off.

They were correct! No one noticed the difference; they were black with some white hair, and they were having fun, just like identical twins do.

The first day, the ship stopped at a port called Boca Rouge, and like the passengers they visited the town, but not before having a huge breakfast.

As they were strolling around, they found a very odd creature. It was very big, but they had never seen one in the forest before. So, they introduced themselves and asked with curiosity, "Hello! What are you? And do you have a name?"

The odd creature did not respond, so they asked again. This time, Dora walked forward first and was very protective. "Sir, my children are asking you a question," Dora said. "Can you understand us?"

Once again, the creature remained silent. "Sir!" Dora said with a motherly voice, "Do you have a name?"

"I do have a name," the creature responded, "but can you see I am napping? I am a native river Alligator, and cats are my favorite meal," the creature revealed. Jimmy, Max, Louie, and Dora took a few steps back and tried to find higher ground.

They spotted a tree and climbed up as fast as they could.

"Oh boy," said Max, "now I know how Felix felt when he first saw us." "I miss that little fella," said Jimmy.

Meanwhile, a tiny frog named Chachi was watching while sitting atop of the alligator's back and said, "Oh! Be quiet, Charlie. You are not that scary. You are so old that you have not moved from this spot in three months after the vets had to rescue you from dying because you ate a tire hub cap."

Charlie snapped back, "Listen little frog, I can just move my body and flip you in the water and eat you!"

"You wouldn't dare!" Responded Chachi with an attitude.

While Charlie the alligator and Chachi the frog were bickering back and forth, Jimmy, Max, Dora, and Louie had jumped out of the tree and left the area.

With no idea where the ship was headed, they waved off the uncertainty, knowing that as long as they were together, they were ready for whatever adventure came their way.

"Who cares where we're going when we're surrounded by good company and a boatload of fun?" Jimmy said with a grin. They all nodded in agreement ready to set sail into the unknown.

The passengers were roaming the town, a beautiful place mainly built for cruise ship tourists. It was Jimmy and Max's first time back on paved streets after living in the forest and they were having a great time.

They saw a few of the crew members heading back to the ship, so they rushed to return before anyone realized that there were four of them. That was enough excitement for one day.

The ship took off to the next city, and they played the same twin game.

Meow, the adventure continues.

How exciting would it be if you could talk to an alligator or a frog? What would you ask them?

Cast of Characters:
Jimmy - Brave Cat
Max - Cautious Cat
Dora - Jimmy and Max's Mom
Louie - Jimmy and Max's Dad
Chachi - Frog
Charlie - Alligator
Felix - Smart Blue Mouse - Old Friend

CHAPTER 4

Meeting Someone Special

The ship was full of adults, and there were no children running around. However, Dora spotted a little girl with a beautiful dress and her hair in a perfect ponytail. Her skin glowed in the moonlight. It was Dora's turn to be on deck, so she got closer to the little girl. Dora wished she could say something to her, as she sensed sadness. When she approached, the little girl's eyes lit up.

"Hi! Little cat! Do you have a name?" The little girl said as she searched for a name tag or collar.

Dora purred and purred around her arms. Her purr was so beautiful that it made a sound like "Dooooraaaaa." The little girl asked again, "Are you saying Dooooooraaaaa? Yes? I will call you Dora!"

Dora was so happy she had almost forgotten how it felt to be caressed and kissed by humans. She really wanted time to stop and stay in the little girl's arms for longer, but she knew that they all had to take turns on the deck. She jumped down as the little girl begged her to stay. When Dora returned to Louie and the kids, she told them about how she sensed sadness in the little girl's eyes. It was Jimmy's turn, so he was curious to see this beautiful girl. He rushed to the deck, and there she was, sitting in the same spot.

"Dora! You're back? Where did you go?" the little girl exclaimed. "No matter, you're back." Jimmy pretended to be his mom, Dora. It was the first time in his life he felt the tiny fingers running through his fur. He wondered about this feeling, it felt so amazing. He was confused and happy at the same time.

He had been around humans before, but never in this way. This was different. He remembered how Felix's wife Sadie talked about feeling love in your stomach, like tiny butterflies flying inside. He stayed a little longer, though it was getting late.

He heard a fatherly voice calling out to the little girl. "Maria, it's time to go to bed, my dear."
"Okay, Daddy, I'm ready," Maria replied.

Jimmy jumped down from her lap and hid in a corner. He saw the man rolling a chair with big wheels, picking Maria up from the lounge chair, and softly placing her in the chair with wheels before rolling her inside. Jimmy couldn't understand what was wrong with Maria; she had perfect human legs.

Jimmy ran down to meet his family, feeling sad and confused with so many emotions that his heart was bursting. "Mom! Mom! Her name is Maria. She is so sweet, and her little hands are like having flower petals touching my fur. Mom! She is not like other kids; she can't walk. Maria had to be carried and set in another chair with wheels. Mom! I have so many questions now. Please tell me whatever you know!"

"Honey! You need to calm down; your heart is beating too fast. Please drink some water. I can explain what you saw," said Dora with a heavy heart.

"Before I left the city, my human mother was a doctor, and I always paid close attention to her conversations with my dad. She had such a soft voice and a kind way of explaining her day at the hospital." A hospital, you know, is like a veterinarian doctor but for humans," Dora joked with a mischievous twinkle in her eye. "Except humans are much fussier patients. You never see a dog demanding organic food or a cat insisting on a separate litter box for each day of the week!"

"Listen to me, the three of you. Sometimes humans have difficulties with their legs, and since they only have two, they need to use what is called a wheelchair. Doctors sometimes have a hard time helping people because of an illness called trauma. I remember my mom crying at night when she couldn't help her patient. So, I would climb on the bed to make her feel better. She used to tell me how much she loved me. Okay, now I am going to cry!" Dora sighed.

"So, we all have to take turns making... What did you say her name was? Maria" feel better, said Dora.

"I believe that our mission on this ship is Maria. We need to find out the reason she is having problems walking and find a way to help her. So, tomorrow after breakfast, we'll find Maria and take turns sitting on her lap and paying close attention to the conversations around her. Maybe if we are smart in doing so, we can find out more about her. Hopefully, she will not notice that there are three boys and a beautiful girl," Dora meowed with a chuckle.

In the morning, Dora went up first and found Maria. She was sitting by a lounge chair under the shade of a canopy having breakfast.

"Dora, you're back! Come sit with me and have some of my eggs. I just love you!" Maria said, beaming with a warm smile.

Dora felt touched by Maria's kindness and generosity. She sat beside Maria, sharing the eggs and enjoying the peaceful morning together. The bond between them grew stronger as they spent time in each other's company.

Dora realized she needed to go and give Max a turn to be up on deck, so she softly slid down.

"Don't go," said Maria. "Please come back!"

Dora hesitated, feeling the tug of Maria's plea. Dora kept running to ensure that Max could meet Maria and spend some time with her. A few minutes later, Max was next to Maria, jumping on her lap. Just like Jimmy, Max felt the warmth of Maria's fingers in his fur and was immediately smitten.

"What an amazing feeling. I can do this for the rest of my life," Max thought to himself.

Maria, being an observant girl, noticed that 'Dora' felt a bit heavier than usual. "What have you been eating? You feel so much heavier. Oh well! Maybe it's our breakfast. Here, we have more eggs," Maria said, offering 'Dora' more food.

Maria's dad called for her, and she replied, "I'm here, Dad!" She begged him to come see something, causing Max to quickly hide to keep their 'twins' game going. Maria excitedly try to introduce her dad to her new friend, but her dad didn't see anyone else around.

"It's okay, Maria," he said reassuringly. "Let's go inside and read a good book together."

Maria was a bit confused, but she was a very obedient little girl, so she went with her dad to the library. Maria took a deep breath as she thought she had been dreaming of meeting Dora.

Night came, and the ship was quiet, while everyone was getting ready for its next stop.

Good night for now. Meow Meow.

-Would you help someone that you just met if you could tell they were really sad?

Cast of Characters:
Jimmy - Brave Cat
Max - Cautious Cat
Dora - Jimmy and Max's mom
Louie - Jimmy and Max's dad
Maria - Little Girl on the Ship
Felix - Smart Blue Mouse - Old Friend

CHAPTER 5

Maria's Nurse

The next morning, the scheduled stop was Memphis, and while all the other passengers were getting off the ship, they noticed that Maria remained onboard. It seemed like her dad was waiting for someone to join them.

The four of them decided that it was more important to stay and watch over Maria. While Maria's dad was settling her back into the lounge chair near the pool, there was beautiful music playing in the background. She looked around, saw Dora and wondered if she was the only one that could see her or if she was imagining her.

This time it was Louie's chance to spend time with Maria. As he slowly approached, Maria's face lit up like a shooting star. "Oh Dora!" She exclaimed, "I was not imagining things, here you are!"

The other three cats were watching how Maria's beautiful face started to illuminate with joy. They noticed that she had changed so much from the first time she met 'Dora'.

In the distance was a tall, beautiful lady in a purple dress with red hair that looked like feathers coming down her back. She smelled like fresh flowers as she was getting closer to Maria. Louie could not move because he was mesmerized by her beauty. She grew closer to Maria, and said with a sweet voice, "Hello Maria, and Hello to you, too, Louie."

"Hello Louie!? What? Wait? How does she know my name? I have never seen this lady before!" he thought, still mesmerized and frozen by her beauty.

"Nice to finally meet you both." She said in a gentle voice. Louie remained confused.

Meanwhile, the other three cats were watching and recognized the sweet lady and her aroma of fresh flowers. "My name is Olivia, and I will be your nurse for the rest of the trip." Olivia turned slowly toward Louie and asked, "Louie, where is everyone else? I know they are here, and you are playing the twins game. Don't worry, no one else can see you; I have placed a spell on everyone on the ship, and they can only see one of you."

And so it begins, our mission to help Maria find her happiness.

And the adventure continues. Meow.

How would you feel if you met a bunch of people that were excited to help you with your own personal problem?

Cast of Characters:
Jimmy - Brave Cat
Max - Cautious Cat
Dora - Jimmy and Max's mom
Louie - Jimmy and Max's dad
Maria - Little Girl on the Ship

CHAPTER 6

Friends to the Rescue

As Olivia evolved, her missions became more complex and involved not only forest creatures but humans as well. Her new assignment was to help Maria heal from a broken heart.

She was in an accident with her dear mom who lost her life, and Maria survived but was left unable to walk. The doctors could not find anything physically wrong with her body or legs, but she refused to make any effort to walk again. She blamed herself for distracting her mom with her constant conversation, causing the accident.

What she didn't know was that the accident happened as a result of the other driver texting while driving and running a red light. Maria was convinced that she was the reason for the accident, making it very difficult to change her mind. Olivia with her magical heart was the only one who would be able to help Maria understand and accept the truth about the accident. Only then would she begin to heal her broken heart.

This was going to get crazier because Olivia had a medical bag, and inside was Felix the mouse and his entire family. "Oh, dear!" said Dora, "This is the happiest day of our lives. We missed you so much, little ones!" Jimmy and Max were jumping and meowing with so much happiness. This was a moment to celebrate for sure. Louie had never met them but had heard so much about them, their blue hair and all, that he was jumping too.

Now that everyone on the ship was under Olivia's spell, Jimmy, Max, Dora, and Louie would be able to be with Maria at the same time. Maria's face couldn't stop smiling.

Maria was emotional, and couldn't understand what was happening, but she was about to. Olivia with her sweet voice and her tall and perfect pose kneeled to Maria's eye level. "Maria, my dear, let me introduce you to my friends. First, these four cats were playing the twins game, but the first one you met was Mama Dora, then you met her sons Max and Jimmy, and finally Louie, their father. Now last but not least, this family is very dear to me, meet Felix the mouse Sadie and their entire family."

Maria had tears rolling down her sweet and soft face, "But I can't," she cried.

"Maria look at me," said Olivia, "you are the only one that can make this happen."

"But, but, you said you have magical powers. Can you make me walk?" asked Maria.

"No." said Olivia, "because you are not sick, you are sad, and sadness can make your mind do very strange things. You have the power, not me. Only you! Maria, look around you, what do you see?"

"I see so many happy faces." Maria sighed.

"And you are right; they are expressing Love for you." Olivia then touched Maria's heart; "Do you feel the LOVE?" She asked.

"Yes!" Maria said with a small, crooked smile.

"And whose face do you see when you look at me?" Olivia asked.

"Maria, I am an Angel and I have magical powers. I made you the only person on this ship that is able to see all these little creatures. Doctors from every part of the world have seen you and they all agree that your body is in perfect health, that your legs are healthy and if you try, you will be able to walk, even run."

"I see my mother! Are you, my mother?" She asked.

Olivia replied, "No, I am not but she is using me to smile back at you. She wants you to be happy, she is watching you from Heaven and is very sad to see you sad. The accident was not your fault; she was actually enjoying your conversation and loved your little voice singing as loud as you could. What song were you singing? Can you remember?"

"Yes, I remember," said Maria.

"Could you teach it to me?" Olivia asked.

Maria said, "Yes, I can try! It goes something like this:

'Happiness, happiness is having friends like you!
I've been down, feeling blue
But then I found, a friend so true
Lost my way, didn't know what to do
Happiness, happiness is having friends like you.'"

"Maria that was beautiful, and we all know that song, it's definitely our favorite too." Said Mama Dora with a big purr.

Maria's face glowed as if fairy dust had landed all over her.

"Maria, can you stand for me? And walk toward me? I promise I will not let you fall; I will hold you tight." Olivia reinforced with her sweet voice, "Nothing will happen to you."

Maria took the first step by lifting her body up from the chair. In her next step she stood up with her eyes fixed on Olivia.

"Good job Maria, that's a good job, now walk towards me." Olivia opened her arms to catch her.

Maria took a step and tried to balance herself, then another, and another until she reached Olivia's soft hands. Olivia hugged her with an enormous, sweet hug and kissed her face.

"Now let's show your dad what you can do, he has been so sad because he's been unable to help you." said Olivia.

All the furry friends were cheering and singing. Of course, no one could hear them or see them except for Maria.

"Daddy, Daddy, look what I can do! I can walk, Daddy, I can walk! Olivia helped me, she has magical powers!" Maria cried tears of happiness.

"No, Maria, the power was all yours. It's called determination and comes from the love inside you." said Olivia

Maria's dad looked at her with tears of joy in his eyes, realizing the strength and determination his daughter had shown. Maria smiled brightly, feeling the love and support surrounding her.

"Maria, I know we haven't had much time together, but I have to get off the ship at our next stop. You have your dad who loves you so very much, and you are going to see so many beautiful places. Who knows, I might even see you again one day. All you have to do is look up to the sky, close your eyes, and call my name." Olivia inspired Maria one last time.

Maria nodded, her eyes shining with gratitude and love for Olivia. She knew that she had found a friend and a source of strength in her, and would always hold her close to her heart. As the ship continued on its journey, Maria and her dad embraced, ready to face whatever adventures lay ahead, knowing that they had each other and the love and support of those who had touched their lives.

Meanwhile, the gang was reunited and ready for another great adventure together like old times.

Meow Meow

Wasn't it wonderful that Maria understood that it was her sadness that was keeping her from walking?

Cast of characters:
Jimmy - Brave Cat
Max - Cautious Cat
Dora - Jimmy and Max's mom
Louie - Jimmy and Max's dad
Maria - Little Girl on the ship Olivia - Angel
Felix - Smart Blue Mouse - Old Friend

CHAPTER 7

The Reunion

Now, the whole gang was together and setting out on a new adventure. They hugged and reminisced about all the amazing miracles that happened including how Dora found Louie. They were destined to be together.

Throughout all their adventures, Felix's children have now grown to be responsible forest creatures. They have had the best life experiences and are very aware of how to save the forest and the animals that live in it. They were a great big family once again.

Olivia, with her new look and angelic duties, was so happy to see all her friends gathering and reminiscing about their adventures. The gang was ready for Olivia's next assignment, which will prove to be a bit more difficult. She would definitely need to be open to meeting this next character. As always, she was up for the challenge.

Olivia noticed that everyone was still in vacation mode due to the many hours of relaxing and overeating on the cruise ship. She made everyone exercise for a while and get their bodies moving again and ready for their next adventure.

After a long walk, Olivia used her magical powers to transport everyone to the new assignment location. This place was in the middle of the mountains with lots of cut trees and a run-down house near a brook .

"Olivia, what is this place? Have you been misbehaving again?" asked Dora.

"No, Dora, I have not misbehaved. This is a very sad case," replied Olivia.

"Please tell us! Should we be worried that an ogre is going to come out and attack everyone or eat us? Or throw us in that well over there?" Louie said pointing.

"The person that lives here has a heart of gold but has lost his way. We are here to help him find his path again." Explained Olivia.

"His name is Mike, please don't be frightened by the way he looks." Olivia continued.

"He used to be a very gentle soul with special powers who cared for everyone, a warrior Angel. Then one day, while on a mission, his superpowers were not enough to complete the assignment, and he lost the person he was caring for. Because of this, he decided to live far away and hidden, never to live around anyone that he could care for, or love. That is the reason he is here, in the middle of nowhere, away from everyone. He is living in the worst conditions as punishment to himself for his mistakes.

"The truth is that he is punishing himself for something that was completely out of his control," Olivia stated sadly. "So here we are on our next assignment. We need to help Mike understand that he can't blame himself for the destiny of others. Everyone has their own journey. We can care for them, we can love them, but we cannot live their lives for them."

"Okay gang! Get ready! I can hear his boots stepping on the dry leaves as he comes closer. Just be aware that he is a very large person that looks a bit scary." She warned.

Everyone hid while leaving Olivia standing on the patio of the house alone. They had experienced scary encounters with a mama bear in the past, so they were not going to come out until Olivia said it was safe. It was after all her mission, and they were just tagging along.

Just then, Mike arrived and saw Olivia. He asked with a deep and demanding voice, "Hmmm, what are you doing here and who sent you?"

"Wait!" said Louie. "Does he know her? Everyone knows her but me?"

Olivia responded with her sweet voice, "I am here to help you, Mike"

"I don't need your help! I don't need anyone's help! Just leave me alone," Mike replied sternly.

"Mike, please sit so we can talk? You've been refusing our help for years, and we can't accept that any longer." Olivia persisted.

"You are wasting your time, Olivia! " Mike yelled.

"I never waste my time, Mike. You need to sit and listen to me, and that is an order!" Olivia demanded with a strong voice.

"Wow! You think you are going to scare me into sitting." Mike scoffed at Olivia. "Yes! Right now! SIT!" Olivia's command echoed with authority while she spread her beautiful wings commanding respect.

At that moment all of the creatures in the woods, regardless of where they were, paused and sat down and obeyed her request. Mike looked into Olivia's eyes with a furious gaze, but Olivia's was stronger and very powerful. Mike started to have a strange feeling and his legs weakened. Slowly, he sat on the first tree trunk he saw.

Mike looked down at the floor, Olivia touched his very dirty face. Just like that, with her magical hands, she cleaned him up and dressed him in more appropriate clothing.

"I'd like to introduce you to my friends, and I would like for you to be nice and polite to them. They are also here to help, but you have scared them so they are hiding. Are you going to be nice?" Olivia asked.

"I will try," responded Mike in a softer voice.

"Okay, everyone, you can come out now." Called out Olivia

The first one to come out was Dora, then everyone else followed.

"Who are these creatures?" asked Mike.

"They are my friends," said Olivia. "They are going to help me make this place livable again for you."

"I don't see how anyone could live here. I'd rather sleep in a tree." Max muttered under his breath.

"Olivia, who is Mike and how come he knows you?" asked Dora.

"Mike is an angel that lost his way," Olivia began. "He was in charge of a special mission many, many years ago, when the world was going through a very sad and hard time. It was a time when people were being taken from their homes for no reason and made to disappear. Mike tried to help, but the world was in too much chaos.

He saw too much pain and suffering, which broke his hearth. All of his powers were not enough to save everyone he loved so much. So, he ran away and gave up on his angelic powers. Mike has refused the Supreme Angels' help and hasn't allowed anyone to enter his heart since then. But we are going to change all that now."

"Oh no!" said Dora. "Can I get near him? Could he understand my voice as you do?"

"Yes, he does," Olivia reassured her.

"Hi Mike! I am Mama Dora! May I sit on your lap?" Dora asked gently.

Mike nodded his head in response.

"It is time for you to find your way back to love and begin helping others again," Dora continued with empathy. "You are very special. Helping others, even if it's just a small gesture, will definitely start mending your broken heart and regain your powers."

Mike listened intently, his gaze softened as he absorbed Dora's words. A glimmer of hope sparked in his eyes as he contemplated the possibility of finding purpose and forgiveness.

"Thank you, Mama Dora," he said softly. "I will try."

"Well, trying is the first step!" exclaimed Dora with a cheerful smile. "Come out, everyone, let's all introduce ourselves to Mike and help him clean up this house."

Olivia was glowing with happiness; her friends were amazing, and once again she had learned so much from Dora. They started the cleanup process as they sang their favorite song:

"Happiness, happiness is having friends like you!"

They all found a special corner in Mike's house and kept him company until he was ready for the Supreme Angelical assignment of his own once again.

While working together, they shared stories and felt their bond grow stronger. These journeys have been a learning experience of mind, body and spirit. With hearts full of love and determination, they looked forward to whatever challenges and joys lay ahead. They were ready for their next adventure.

Meow, till our next adventure!

Did you enjoy the journey to happiness? Do you have a favorite story?

Cast of Characters:
Jimmy - Brave Cat
Max - Cautious Cat
Dora - Jimmy and Max's mom
Louie - Jimmy and Max's dad Olivia - Angel
Mike - The Lost Angel
Felix - Smart Blue Mouse - Old Friend

Moral:

The moral of the story is that no matter how lost or broken we may feel, there is always hope for healing and forgiveness. Through the support and love of friends and family, we can find our way back to ourselves and rediscover our purpose. It teaches us the importance of reaching out for help when we need it, and the power of friendship and compassion in overcoming obstacles. Additionally, the story emphasizes the transformative power of kindness and understanding, showing that even the toughest hearts can be softened by empathy and connection.

Printed in the United States
by Baker & Taylor Publisher Services